THE ADVENTURES OF
PIGGY BOTTOM

ISBN: 9798218552343

LIFE IS SHORT.
BE UNAPOLOGETICALLY YOU.

I'M A NASTY PIG, I'VE GOT A SMUDGE.
IT'S ON MY LEG FROM PACKING FUDGE.

I LOVE PIG PLAY, I'M NOT PURE.
AM I TOO NASTY? I'M NOT SURE.

I'M A NASTY PIG. AFTER HANDBALL,
I DON'T RECALL LAST NIGHT AT ALL.

4

I LOVE PIG PLAY, I'M NOT PURE.
AM I TOO NASTY? I'M NOT SURE.

I'M A NASTY PIG, I'M HERE WITH OTTER.
I JUST NOW GOT BLOWN IN THE WATER.

I LOVE PIG PLAY, I'M NOT PURE.
AM I TOO NASTY? I'M NOT SURE.

I'M A NASTY PIG, THAT MADE ME GRIN.
I'LL TOSS YOUR SALAD, YOU TOSS MINE AGAIN.

I LOVE PIG PLAY, I'M NOT PURE.
AM I TOO NASTY? I'M NOT SURE.

I'M A NASTY PIG. THIS DOG'S OKAY,
BUT A BIT OF CHILI WOULD MAKE MY DAY.

I LOVE PIG PLAY, I'M NOT PURE.
AM I TOO NASTY? I'M NOT SURE.

I'M A NASTY PIG, CREAM PIE'S A TREAT!
AS MUCH FUN TO MAKE AS IT IS TO EAT!

I LOVE PIG PLAY, I'M NOT PURE.
AM I TOO NASTY? I'M NOT SURE.

I'M A NASTY PIG, OUT O' CONTROL.
I STAYED TOO LONG IN THE GLORY HOLE.

I LOVE PIG PLAY, I'M NOT PURE.
AM I TOO NASTY? I'M NOT SURE.

"OTTER, DEAR FRIEND, YOU'LL TELL ME THE TRUTH.
HAS MY BEHAVIOR BECOME UNCOUTH?"

"OH, PIGGY, YOU'RE A NASTY MESS,
BUT THAT DOESNT MEAN WE LOVE YOU LESS."

"BEAR, LET ME ASK. WHAT DO YOU THINK?
HAVE I JUST GONE TOO FAR WITH KINK?"

"OH WAY PAST THAT, AND BEYOND TOO FAR,
BUT WE ALL LOVE YOU THE WAY YOU ARE."

I'M THE NASTIEST PIG YOU'LL EVER FIND.
I'LL RUB YOUR HEAD, THEN BLOW YOUR MIND.

I EAT CREAM PIE FOR BRUNCH AND LUNCH,
THEN WASH IT DOWN WITH DONKEY PUNCH.

I'M A DIRTY PIG, I'M A FILTHY SWINE,
THIS GOLDEN SHOWER IS JUST DIVINE.

I LOVE PIG PLAY, I'M NOT PURE.
AM I TOO NASTY?

OH FOR SURE!

www.ingramcontent.com/pod-product-compliance
Lightning Source LLC
Chambersburg PA
CBHW070216010826
48976CB00014B/2647